About This Book

Title: On the Tracks

Step: 2

Word Count: 105

Skills in Focus: Initial and Final Blends

Tricky Words: like, these, through, people, them, for, now

Ideas for Using this Book

Before Reading:
- **Comprehension:** Look at the title and cover image together. Have you traveled on a train? What was it like? Ask the reader to make a prediction.
- **Accuracy:** Practice the tricky words listed on Page 1.
- **Phonemic Awareness:** Look at the title and help readers blend the sounds. Practice taking apart and putting together the sounds in the word *track*. How many sounds are in the word *track*? What is the first sound? Second sound? Third sound? End sound? Call attention to the initial blend. Offer other examples that will appear in the book: *stop, stand, last*.

During Reading:
- Have the reader point under each word as they read it.
- **Decoding:** If stuck on a word, help readers say each sound and blend it together smoothly.
- **Comprehension:** Prompt readers to notice how the setting changes throughout the story. Invite them to add to or change their prediction from before reading.

After Reading:
Discuss the book. Some ideas for questions:
- What is the setting of the story? How does it change? Use picture clues.
- What do you think the train likes about its job? Use details from the story.

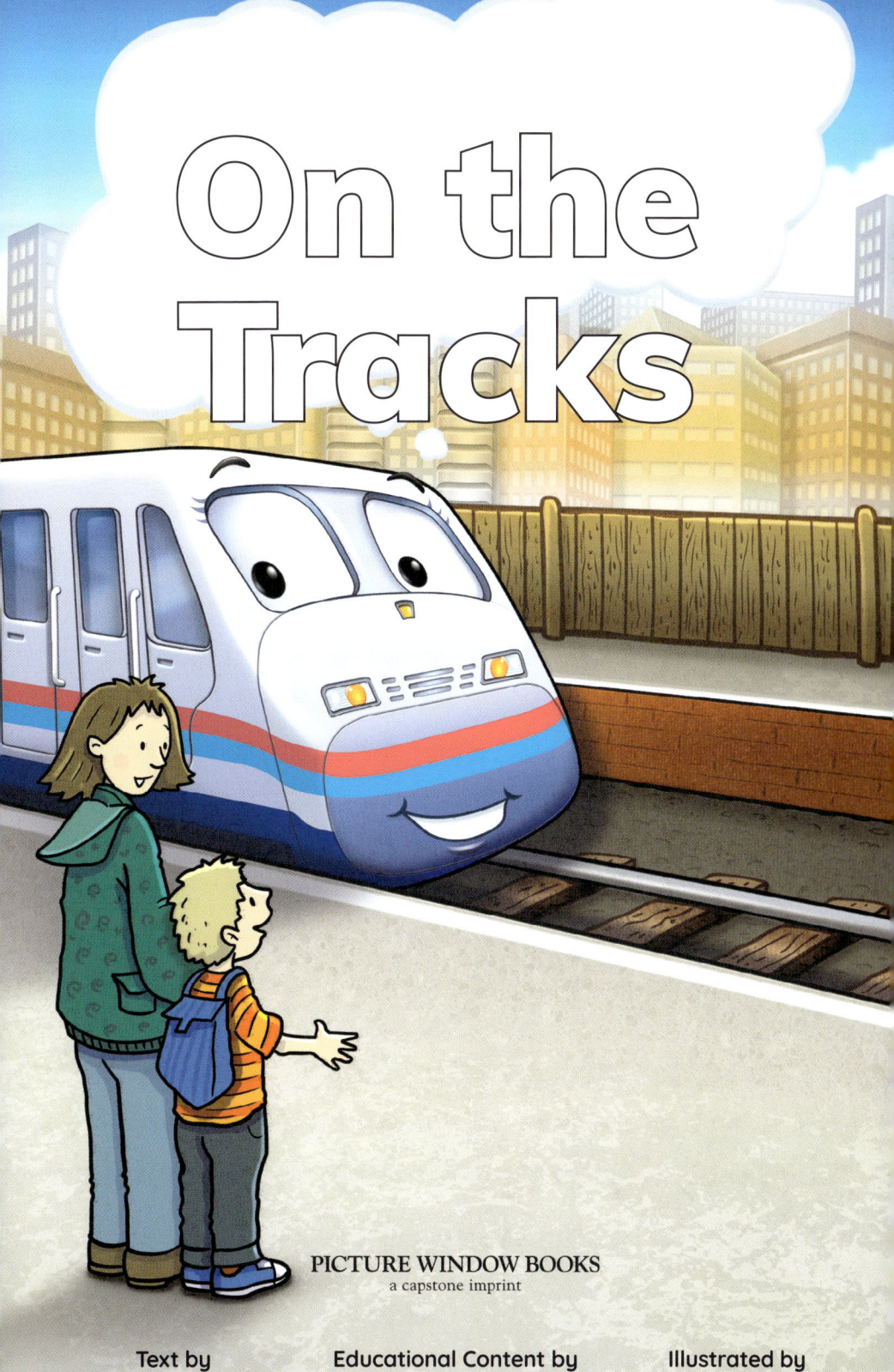

I pick people up. I am fast!

I help people get to the next stop.

I pick up lots of people.

I go past lots of spots.

I stop at red flags. I pick up moms, dads, and kids.

On this trip, I get people through hills.

I will grab these people next. Step on up!

Now I am at my last stop.

I can rest a bit.

More Ideas:

Phonemic Awareness Activity

Practicing Final Blends:
Tell students you will say a story word with the final blend, *st*. Begin with the word *rest*, r-e-s-t. They will substitute the initial sound to make a new word. Ask them to change the /r/ to /b/, making the word *best*. Continue substituting the initial sound to make a new word. Repeat with the next word list.

Suggested words:
- rest, best, nest, test, west
- last, cast, fast, past

Extended Learning Activity

Setting:
The setting of the story changes as the train travels from stop to stop. Use picture clues to describe the various settings. Provide readers with a sheet of paper folded into sections (as many as will appropriately challenge the reader). Draw a story setting in each section.

Optional: Challenge readers to label their pictures.

Published by Picture Window Books,
an imprint of Capstone
1710 Roe Crest Drive,
North Mankato, Minnesota 56003
capstonepub.com

On the Tracks was originally published as
City Train, copyright 2013 Stone Arch Books.

Copyright © 2024 by Capstone.
All rights reserved. No part of this publication may be reproduced in whole or in part, or stored in a retrieval system, or transmitted in any form or by any means, electronic, mechanical, photocopying, recording, or otherwise, without written permission of the publisher.

Library of Congress Cataloging-in-Publication Data is available on the Library of Congress website.

ISBN: 9780756595081 (hardback)
ISBN: 9780756584016 (paperback)
ISBN: 9780756583996 (eBook PDF)

Printed and bound in the USA. 5757